HOWL FOR HALLOWEEN!

Based on the teleplay "The Pups and the Ghost Pirate" by Ursula Ziegler Sullivan

Illustrated by Nate Lovett

A GOLDEN BOOK • NEW YORK

randomhousekids.com

ISBN 978-0-399-55873-3

Printed in the United States of America

10 9 8 7 6 5 4 3 2 1

It was Halloween at the Lookout, and the PAW Patrol was excitedly preparing for the big night.

"Dressing up in costume is my favorite part of Halloween," said Princess Skye.

"My favorite part is trick-or-treating!" said Pirate Zuma. *"Arr!"*

But there was one thing they agreed on: they were both looking forward to Cap'n Turbot's ghost ship party!

"They say the ship is haunted," said Skye.
"It sounds super scary."

"Aww, that's only scary if you believe in ghosts," Zuma replied.

Suddenly, they heard a spooky wailing sound, and a ghost fluttered down next to Zuma! The pirate pup yelped and jumped into the air.

"That's not a real ghost," Skye said with a giggle.
"That's just Chase hanging a decoration."
"Told you there's no such thing as ghosts," Zuma
said, though he was shaking.

Outside the Lookout, Rocky, Marshall, and Rubble had found a huge pumpkin to carve. Rocky cut the top with his Super Jack-o'-Lantern Scooper, and Marshall tried to pull it off. He tugged and tugged until it popped off the pumpkin . . .

Meanwhile, Cap'n Turbot welcomed his first guests to the old pirate ship. Mayor Goodway and Chickaletta, Katie and Cali, and Mr. Porter and his grandson, Alex, all wore wonderful costumes. Mr. Porter had brought delicious Halloween cookies, and everyone told Cap'n Turbot they liked the spooky way he had decorated the boat.

"Thank you," he said. "Just trying to be the host with the most ghosts. Legend has it that this pirate vessel once sailed the waters of Adventure Bay with a ghost crew! *Mwah-ha-ha-ha!*"

Alex was a little scared.
He tugged at his grandpa's
sleeve. "Is the ship really
haunted?" he asked.
"No," said
Mr. Porter. "It's fun
to play at being
scared sometimes.
There's no such
thing as ghosts."

But if there were no ghosts on board,
Mr. Porter wondered, who had eaten all
his Halloween cookies?

And Katie wondered what was
making that spooky moaning sound.

Later, while Cali was chasing a pesky seagull around the ship, she accidentally pulled on a rope that raised a sail.

Mayor Goodway was spooked. "Why is that sail going up on its own?" she asked.

Then the ship started to move! As the boat sailed away, the gangplank collapsed and Cap'n Turbot fell into the water! The pirate ship was headed out to sea—with no one at the helm!

"I seem to have misplaced my glasses in the ocean," Cap'n Turbot said, rushing to climb back on board. But without his glasses, he couldn't steer the boat.

This was a job for the PAW Patrol!
Mr. Porter called for help, and Ryder
assembled the team.

"Strange things are happening at
Cap'n Turbot's Halloween party,"
he said. "Zuma, I need you and
your hovercraft to catch up with the
runaway ship."

"Let's dive in!" barked the pirate pup.

"Skye, I need you and your helicopter to help slow
down the ship," Ryder added. "And, Marshall, I need
you to ride in Skye's harness to help lower the sails."
The team was ready for a ruff-ruff rescue!

Ryder and Zuma raced across the water as Skye zoomed through the air, carrying Marshall. When they reached the pirate ship, Skye slowed down and Marshall swung into the crow's nest! Everyone cheered when Marshall lowered the sails.

At the same time, Ryder and Zuma raced alongside the ship. Ryder climbed out of his ATV and onto a ladder. But when Zuma jumped, he missed and splashed into the sea!

Luckily, he had propellers on his Pup Pack. He turned them on and shot out of the water—right into Ryder's arms!

The pirate ship was rocking
and turning through the waves
as if someone was sailing it!
"A ghost must be doing it,"
said Alex. "That is so cool!"

Alex might have thought being on a ghost ship was cool, but Ryder wasn't convinced. "There's got to be a simple explanation for all this," he said. "Let's check out the steering wheel."

But Zuma and Marshall didn't budge. "Oh," said Zuma, looking around for ghosts. "You meant us, too."

When Ryder, Zuma, and Marshall went to investigate, they made a surprising discovery: Chickaletta was perched on the wheel, turning it back and forth!

"There's your Halloween ghost," Ryder said, laughing. Zuma and Marshall sighed with relief.

But as Ryder was taking Chickaletta back to Mayor Goodway, a spooky moan came from behind some old barrels. Everyone was scared, but Ryder boldly walked toward the kegs.

Marshall and Zuma tried to stop him. "Ryder, don't!" they pleaded.

Ryder looked into the shadows and found . . .

. . . Wally the walrus napping behind the barrels!

"Wally's snores were echoing back here, which made the spooky sound," Ryder said.

When Mr. Porter looked, he saw cookie crumbs on the deck. "And it was Wally who ate all the cookies!"

Just then, Callie ran by, chasing the seagull. Once again, she accidentally raised the sail—but this time, the others saw it happen.

"Chickaletta was our secret captain. Wally the walrus made the ghostly sounds. And Callie raised the sails," Ryder said. He had solved all the mysteries! He even helped Cap'n Turbot find his glasses . . . in his pocket!

Once they all got to dry land, they moved the party to the Lookout. There were games and treats for everyone. And best of all, the fun was ghost-free! Then Rocky looked up and saw something amazing.

A glowing pirate ship seemed to be floating across the full moon!

"I'm sure there's a simple explanation—I just don't know what it is!" said Ryder. "Happy Halloween, everyone!"